I0663204

A Little Hero

Innocence, First Love,
and the Confusion of Growing Up

A Modern Translation

Adapted for the Contemporary Reader

Fyodor Dostoevsky

Translated by Tim Zengerink

Table of Contents

Preface - Message to the Reader

What If You Could Help Rebuild the Greatest Library in Human History?

Thousands of years ago, the Library of Alexandria stood as the crown jewel of human achievement — a sanctuary where the collected wisdom of every known civilization was gathered, preserved, and shared freely.

And then, it was lost.

Through fire, conquest, and the slow erosion of time, humanity lost not just books — but ideas, dreams, discoveries, and stories that could have changed the world forever.

Today, the Library of Alexandria lives again — and you are invited to be a part of its restoration.

Our mission is simple yet profound:

To rebuild the greatest library the world has ever known, and to translate all timeless works into every language and dialect, so that no seeker of knowledge is ever left behind again.

By joining our movement to rebuild the modern Library of Alexandria, you become part of an unprecedented mission:

- **Unlimited Access to the Greatest Audiobooks & eBooks Ever Written:**

  Instantly explore thousands of legendary works—Plato, Shakespeare, Jane Austen, Leo Tolstoy, and countless more. All instantly available to read or listen, placing a complete literary universe at your fingertips.

- **Beautiful Paperback & Deluxe Editions at Printing Cost**

  Own any title as an elegant paperback, deluxe hardcover, or stunning collectible boxset—offered to you at true printing cost, delivered straight to your door. Build your personal Library of Alexandria, crafted for beauty, built for durability, and worthy of proud display.

- **Fresh Translations for Modern Readers—in Every Language & Dialect**

  Enjoy timeless masterpieces reimagined in clear, contemporary language—no more outdated phrases or obscure references. Alongside the original versions, we're tirelessly translating these classics into every language and dialect imaginable, ensuring accessibility and understanding across cultures and generations.

- **Join a Global Renaissance of Literature & Knowledge**

  You directly support expanding our library, publishing deluxe editions at true cost, translating works into all global languages, and bringing humanity's greatest stories to people everywhere. By joining today, you're not just preserving a legacy of masterpieces; you set in motion a powerful wave of literary accessibility.

Become a Torchbearer of Knowledge.

Join us for free now at **LibraryofAlexandria.com**

Together, we will ensure that the light of human wisdom never fades again.

With gratitude and a shared love of knowledge,

The Modern Library of Alexandria Team

Visit:

www.libraryofalexandria.com

Or scan the code below:

Introduction

A Glimpse into the Heart of a Child: First Emotions and the Mystery of Maturity

Fyodor Dostoevsky's A Little Hero stands as one of his most unique and understated short stories—less a moral or philosophical treatise than a gentle, introspective vignette capturing the world as seen through the eyes of a child. Written in 1849 during the author's imprisonment in the Peter and Paul Fortress, this semi-autobiographical tale offers a rare glimpse into the young emotional consciousness of a boy witnessing the strange, adult world of aristocratic flirtation, social performance, and unspoken tensions. In its simplicity and sensitivity, A Little Hero reveals Dostoevsky's deep understanding of childhood psychology and the formative power of early emotional experiences.

Unlike Dostoevsky's later, more complex novels which plunge into moral chaos, psychological torment, and spiritual revelation, A Little Hero invites readers to slow down and remember the innocence and confusion of youth. The story follows a nameless boy—timid, observant, and impressionable—as he attends a ball in a noble household. There, surrounded by adults engaging in banter, courtship, and elaborate social rituals, the child undergoes a quiet inner awakening. He feels shame, joy, fear, curiosity, and most powerfully, the first stirrings of romantic affection toward a young lady who shows him kindness and attention. These experiences, though seemingly mundane from an adult perspective, are monumental in the child's inner world, shaping his understanding of selfhood, affection, and social hierarchy.

In A Little Hero, Dostoevsky explores the beginnings of emotional identity—how love, admiration, and embarrassment begin to mold a young person's character. It is a story about thresholds: between childhood and adolescence, imagination and reality, innocence and awakening. With remarkable delicacy, Dostoevsky presents not a critique of society or a philosophical argument, but a window into the silent emotional revolutions that shape who we become.

A Child Among Adults:
Social Masks, Affection, and the Making of Memory

What makes A Little Hero so affecting is its restraint. The boy does not fully understand what he is witnessing—his observations are clouded by awe, self-consciousness, and confusion. He sees adults laughing, teasing, whispering, and moving with an ease and elegance that he both admires and fears. His perspective is not critical, but curious; not cynical, but enchanted. Yet through his eyes, the reader discerns the artificiality, the performative nature, and the latent cruelty of adult social life. The aristocrats at the ball are charming, but also self-serving. Their interactions are layered with irony and flirtation that the child can only partially decode.

It is in this atmosphere of superficial delight and underlying ambiguity that the boy's emotional journey unfolds. The object of his affection—a graceful young woman who takes notice of him—is not a manipulative figure, but a fleeting beacon of attention and warmth. Her kindness gives the boy a sense of validation, and his resulting attachment is deep and sincere. In her gaze, he feels seen. In her touch, he finds courage. And when he sees her later interacting with a man closer to her age, he experiences for the first time the pain of jealousy and exclusion. It is this sequence of emotional discoveries—love, belonging, loss—that constitutes the hero's journey, not through physical adventure, but through inner transformation.

Dostoevsky's title, A Little Hero, is gently ironic. The boy does nothing outwardly grand; there is no battle fought, no victory won. His heroism is interior— a brave confrontation with unfamiliar feelings and social dynamics. In this sense, the story is a deeply modern narrative, portraying emotional growth as the true arena of character development. It affirms that the heart's early education, often neglected in literature and society, is where much of our lifelong strength and vulnerability are born.

This modern translation preserves the warmth, clarity, and emotional subtlety of Dostoevsky's original text while updating the language to ensure accessibility for contemporary readers. Care has been taken to retain the innocence of tone and the richness of the boy's perceptions, capturing both the sweetness and the melancholy of his brief moment of affection and heartbreak.

In conclusion, A Little Hero is a tender, introspective celebration of childhood consciousness. It is not a dramatic tale, but a deeply human one. It reminds us that our earliest feelings—our first infatuation, our first pangs of envy, our first silent heartbreak—are not minor episodes, but the foundations of identity. Dostoevsky, with remarkable sensitivity, honors the emotional truth of a child's experience, giving it the dignity it so often lacks. In doing so, he reminds us that even the smallest hearts carry the seeds of greatness, and that sometimes, heroism begins in learning to feel.

A Little Hero

A story

At that time, I was almost eleven years old. In July, I was sent to spend the holidays in a village near Moscow with a relative of mine, whom I'll call T. His house was packed with guests—fifty or maybe even more. I'm not sure; I didn't count. The place was full of noise and laughter. It felt like one long, endless celebration. It seemed as if our host had decided to spend his enormous fortune as fast as he could, and not too long ago, he succeeded in doing just that, leaving nothing behind.

New visitors arrived all the time. Since Moscow was nearby, anyone leaving made room for others to take their place, and the never-ending party continued. One festivity followed another, with no sign of stopping. There were group rides around the area, trips to the forest or the river, picnics, outdoor dinners, and suppers on the grand terrace of the house. The terrace was lined with rows of stunning flowers, their scent filling the fresh night air. The lights on the terrace made the ladies, many of whom were already quite beautiful, appear even more radiant. Their faces glowed with excitement from the day's adventures, their eyes sparkled, and their lively conversations and bursts of laughter made everything seem magical. There was dancing, music, and singing. If the weather turned cloudy, there were living pictures, charades, and plays. Even private theatrical performances were organized. There were also people who told fascinating stories, made witty remarks, or were simply great to talk to.

Some people stood out more than others. Of course, there was gossip and backbiting—it seemed the world couldn't function without them. Without such drama, millions of people would probably die of boredom, like flies. But at the time, I was only eleven, and my interests were completely different. Either I didn't notice those things, or I didn't understand them. It wasn't until later that some of those moments came back to me. At the time, all my childish eyes could see was the bright and exciting side of things—the energy, the splendor, and the commotion. Seeing and hearing all this for the first time had such a strong impact on me that, for the first few days, I felt completely dazed, my little head spinning with all the excitement.

I keep mentioning my age because I was just a child—nothing more than a child. Many of the lovely ladies treated me with affection, not even thinking about my age. But strangely, I started to feel something I didn't fully understand. Something new was stirring in my heart—something I had never known before. For some reason, it made my heart beat faster and filled me with a kind of warmth. Sometimes my face would suddenly flush with heat. At times, I felt embarrassed or even annoyed by the privileges that came with being a child. Other times, I was filled with a sense of wonder. I would slip away to a quiet corner to sit alone, as if I needed a moment to breathe and remember something—something I thought I had always known but had suddenly forgotten. Without it, I felt I couldn't show my face to anyone or even exist.

At last, I began to feel as if I were keeping a secret from everyone. But I couldn't have talked about it even if I wanted to—I was just a boy, and the thought of sharing it filled me with shame. Before long, despite all the excitement around me, I started to feel lonely. There were other children there, but they were either much older or much younger than me, and I didn't feel like spending time with them. Of course, none of this would have mattered if I hadn't been in such an unusual situation. To the lovely ladies around me, I was just a little boy they could pamper and play with, almost like a doll. One of them, in particular, a beautiful woman with thick, luxurious hair like I had never seen before—

and probably never will again—seemed determined never to leave me alone. I was embarrassed by her attention, but she seemed to find endless amusement in teasing me, laughing at the reactions she provoked from others, which only added to her fun.

She was a fair-haired woman with a kind of beauty that drew everyone's eyes the moment she entered a room. She was nothing like the delicate, shy, and pale girls I'd imagined from stories—those soft, quiet types who reminded one of white mice or the daughters of pastors. She wasn't very tall and had a slightly plump figure, but her features were soft, delicate, and perfectly formed. Her face seemed alive with energy, as if she were made of fire. Her big, blue eyes sparkled like diamonds, full of life and light, and I wouldn't trade them for the darkest and most enchanting black eyes anyone might dream of. In fact, my golden-haired beauty was every bit as stunning as the famous brunette described by a great poet, who declared in one of his poems that he would gladly break every bone in his body just to touch the edge of her cloak.

On top of that, my charming blonde was the liveliest, most playful person I'd ever met. She had a laugh as bright as the first light of dawn, like a rosebud blooming in the sun while still covered with cool drops of dew. Despite being married for five years, she was as lighthearted and mischievous as a child. There was always laughter on her lips, fresh and full of life.

I remember that the day after I arrived, they were preparing for a private play. The drawing room was packed with people—there wasn't a single empty seat. Since I came in late, I had no choice but to stand. The play was so entertaining that I kept moving closer and closer without even realizing it. Before I knew it, I was at the front, leaning on the back of an armchair where a lady was sitting. It turned out to be my blonde enchantress, though we hadn't yet been introduced. I found myself staring at her beautiful shoulders, soft and white as milk, though honestly, I wasn't thinking about whether they were lovely or not. For all I cared, I might have been staring at an older woman's brightly colored cap in the front row.

Sitting next to my blonde was an older woman, one of those spinsters who, I later noticed, always seem to sit near young and pretty women, especially the ones who are open and friendly to others. But that's beside the point. This particular lady caught me staring and leaned over to whisper something to my blonde. Instantly, the blonde woman turned around. Her glowing eyes flashed in the dim light, and I was so startled by her gaze that I jumped, as if I'd been burned. She smiled, and her beauty lit up the room.

"Do you like the play?" she asked, looking directly at me with a mix of shyness and teasing in her expression.

"Yes," I replied, still staring at her in a kind of amazement that seemed to amuse her.

"But why are you standing? You'll get tired. Can't you find a seat?"

"That's the problem—I can't," I said, focusing more on my complaint than on her sparkling eyes. I felt genuinely relieved to have found someone kind enough to listen to my troubles. "I looked everywhere, but all the chairs are taken," I added, as if blaming her for the lack of seating.

"Come here," she said suddenly, acting on impulse, as if every wild idea that popped into her head had to be carried out at once. "Come here and sit on my knee."

"On your knee?" I repeated, startled. I'd already started feeling embarrassed about being treated like a child, and this woman had gone far beyond the others in making me feel that way. On top of that, I had always been shy, especially around women, and lately, that shyness had only grown stronger.

"Why not on my knee? What's stopping you?" she insisted, laughing harder and harder, until she was giggling uncontrollably. Whether she was laughing at her own silly idea or at my obvious discomfort, I had no clue. But that seemed to be exactly what she wanted.

I felt my face flush, and in my embarrassment, I glanced around, looking for an escape. But before I could make a move, she grabbed my hand to stop me from leaving. To my utter surprise and confusion, she held my hand tightly in her warm, playful fingers and suddenly began pinching my fingers, hard enough to hurt. I tried my best not to cry out, but the pain made me pull ridiculous faces as I struggled to stay silent. I was overwhelmed with confusion, shock, and even a bit of horror at the idea that someone could be so absurd and mean-spirited—pinching a boy's fingers in front of everyone for no reason at all. My face must have shown just how upset I was, because she laughed even harder, right in my face, as if she were losing her mind. At the same time, she kept pinching my fingers harder and harder, clearly enjoying the whole ridiculous game and taking pleasure in embarrassing and confusing me.

I was trapped. My face burned with humiliation, especially since nearly everyone around us had turned to look. Some stared in confusion, while others were laughing, realizing that the beautiful woman was up to some sort of mischief. I wanted desperately to scream—she was wringing my fingers with so much force it felt unbearable—but I was determined to endure it. I didn't want to cry out and cause a big scene, which would have been even worse. In utter desperation, I finally started trying to pull my hand away with all my strength, but she was much stronger than I was. Eventually, I couldn't take it anymore and let out a loud cry. That was exactly what she had been waiting for! As soon as I yelled, she let go of my hand and turned away as if nothing had happened.

She acted so innocent, as though it wasn't her who had caused all the commotion but someone else entirely. She reminded me of a mischievous schoolboy who, as soon as the teacher's back is turned, pulls some prank—pinching a weaker child, flicking their ear, or giving them a quick shove—only to immediately act as if nothing had happened. The moment the teacher looks back, the prankster buries his nose in his book and starts reciting his lesson, pretending to be the perfect student, leaving the frustrated teacher unsure of what to do.

That was how our strange acquaintance began, and from that evening on, she never left me alone. She tormented me endlessly, without the slightest care or conscience, becoming my personal tyrant and tormentor. The most ridiculous part of her teasing was that she pretended to be madly in love with me and delighted in embarrassing me in front of everyone. For someone like me, wild and sensitive as I was, her antics were so irritating and upsetting that I was often driven to the brink of tears. There were even moments when I was so overwhelmed by her tricks that I seriously considered fighting back against my mischievous tormentor.

My awkwardness and clear frustration only seemed to encourage her more. She had no pity, and I had no way of escaping her. The constant laughter that followed us everywhere, which she expertly provoked, only spurred her on to try new pranks. Eventually, though, people started to think she was taking things a bit too far. Looking back now, I realize she really did act outrageously toward a child like me.

But that was just her nature. She was spoiled in every possible way. Later, I learned more about her and her husband. He was a very short, very fat man with a red face, incredibly wealthy, and always busy with his work. He was constantly on the move and could never stay in one place for more than a couple of hours. Every day, he went to Moscow—sometimes twice—and always claimed it was for business.

His face was lively and cheerful, with an air of friendliness that never seemed forced. He not only loved his wife but adored her to the point of absolute devotion. He treated her like a goddess, indulging her every whim and giving her everything she wanted without hesitation.

He never restricted her in anything. She had a wide circle of friends, both men and women. For one thing, almost everyone liked her, and for another, she wasn't particularly picky about who she made friends with. However, her personality was deeper and more complex than it might have seemed from the way she acted. Out of all her friends, she was closest to a young woman who was a distant relative and happened to be part of our group. The two of them shared a deep and unique bond, one of those friendships that sometimes form between two very different people. One of them was more serious, pure, and thoughtful, while the other, with a humble and generous spirit, willingly admired and yielded to her friend, aware of her qualities and cherishing the friendship as something precious. This created a relationship full of tenderness and respect—on one side, love and endless patience; on the other, love mixed with admiration, almost like reverence. There was also a longing to understand each other better and grow closer with each passing moment.

The two women were the same age, but they couldn't have been more different, starting with their appearances. Madame M. was also very beautiful, but there was something unique about her beauty that set her apart from other pretty women. Her face had a rare quality that immediately won people's affection—or, more accurately, inspired a warm, noble feeling of kindness in everyone who met her. Some people are simply blessed with faces like that. When she was around, it felt like everyone became better, kinder, and more open. At the same time, her large, expressive eyes—so full of energy and life—always seemed anxious, as if expecting something unpleasant or threatening at any moment. This unusual timidity sometimes gave her calm, gentle features a touch of sadness, like the serene faces of Italian Madonnas. Looking at her, it was hard not to feel a deep sadness, as though she reminded you of some hidden sorrow of your own.

Her pale, delicate face, with its perfectly proportioned and elegant features, often carried a silent sorrow. Yet, there were fleeting moments when her expression softened, showing a glimpse of innocence and trust, almost like the joy of early childhood. Her hesitant, uncertain smile stirred a deep sympathy in everyone, drawing out a kind of warmth and concern that even strangers felt toward her. Despite her quiet and reserved nature, she was attentive and loving toward anyone in need. Some women are like angels of mercy in life. They seem to know instinctively when someone is hurting and are always ready to help. They carry a patience and love that is boundless, offering comfort and hope to anyone who seeks it, without ever making them feel like a burden. Few people understand just how much compassion and forgiveness some women's hearts can hold.

These women are often quietly suffering themselves, hiding their pain from others, for deep sadness rarely reveals itself openly. Yet they are fearless in the face of another's sorrow, no matter how deep or ugly it might be. To them, anyone who comes seeking help deserves it, and it feels as though they were born for acts of heroism. Madame M. was one of these rare souls. She was tall, graceful, and slender. Her movements could be unpredictable—sometimes slow, smooth, and dignified, while at other times, quick and almost childlike. Yet there was a delicate humility in the way she moved, a kind of vulnerability that never begged for protection but seemed to quietly invite understanding.

I have already mentioned how the relentless teasing from the mischievous, fair-haired lady embarrassed and bewildered me, wounding me deeply. But there was another secret reason, strange and foolish, which I kept hidden and dreaded as if it were a skeleton in the closet. Just thinking about it, as I sat alone in some dark, mysterious corner where her mocking blue-eyed gaze couldn't reach me, made me feel overwhelmed with confusion, shame, and fear. The truth was—I was in love. That might sound ridiculous, perhaps impossible, but why else, out of all the faces around me, was hers the only one that held my attention? Why was it that only she caught my eye, even though I wasn't interested in watching or getting to know women at that age?

This feeling came over me most often on evenings when bad weather kept us indoors. Those nights, I would sit quietly in a corner of the large drawing room, with nothing to do, feeling completely alone. Hardly anyone spoke to me except the ladies who teased me, and I was unbearably bored. In those moments, my gaze would wander to the people around me, listening to their conversations—most of which I couldn't even understand. But somehow, the gentle smile, kind eyes, and beautiful face of Madame M. always seemed to draw me in. She was the focus of my fascination, and the strange, sweet feelings she inspired stayed with me long after.

For hours, I couldn't look away from her. I studied her every gesture and movement, listening intently to the soft, rich tones of her silvery voice, even though it was slightly muffled. But what struck me most was a deep sense of curiosity mixed with my timid admiration, as if I were on the edge of discovering some great mystery.

Nothing upset me more than being teased in front of Madame M. Her laughter, which I thought of as part of the general mockery, humiliated me terribly. Whenever the whole room burst into laughter at my expense, and Madame M. couldn't help but join in, I felt such despair and misery that I would run away from my tormentor, retreating upstairs to hide for the rest of the day. I couldn't bring myself to face anyone in the drawing room after that. I didn't fully understand my feelings of shame and agitation—it all happened without me realizing what was going on. I had hardly ever spoken a word to Madame M., and I certainly wouldn't have dared to.

But one evening, after an unbearable day, I returned with the rest of the group from an outing. I was utterly exhausted and made my way home through the garden. As I walked down a secluded path, I saw Madame M. sitting alone on a bench. She seemed to have chosen that quiet spot on purpose. Her head was bowed, and she was absentmindedly twisting her handkerchief in her fingers. She was so lost in thought that she didn't notice me until I was standing right in front of her.

Noticing me, she quickly stood up from the bench, turned away, and I saw her hastily wipe her eyes with her handkerchief. She had been crying. After drying her eyes, she smiled at me and began walking back to the house with me. I don't remember what we talked about, but she kept sending me away on little errands—to pick a flower or to see who was riding in the next path. Each time I walked away, she would immediately press the handkerchief to her eyes again, wiping away stubborn tears that kept welling up from her heart and falling from her sad eyes.

I soon realized I was bothering her, as she kept finding reasons to send me away. She knew I had noticed, but she couldn't help herself, and that made my heart ache even more for her. I felt angry with myself, almost desperate. I blamed my clumsiness and inability to help, but at the same time, I didn't know how to leave her without making it obvious that I'd seen her pain. So I stayed by her side, feeling lost and helpless, unable to say anything meaningful to break the awkwardness of our sparse conversation.

This meeting left such a deep impression on me that I spent the entire evening watching Madame M. with intense curiosity, unable to take my eyes off her. Twice, she caught me staring. The second time, she noticed and gave me a small smile. It was the only time she smiled all evening. Her face was still pale, and the sadness had not left her expression.

She spent most of the evening talking with an unpleasant, quarrelsome old lady who was disliked by everyone because of her habit of gossiping and spying on people. However, everyone was afraid of her and felt they had to treat her politely, despite their dislike.

At ten o'clock, Madame M.'s husband arrived. Until that moment, I had been watching her closely, never looking away from her sorrowful face. When her husband appeared unexpectedly, I saw her flinch, and her pale face suddenly turned as white as a handkerchief. It was so obvious that others noticed it too. I overheard bits of conversation and gathered that Madame M. was not entirely happy. People said her husband was as jealous as an Arab, not out of love, but out of pride.

He considered himself a thoroughly modern man, proud of keeping up with the latest ideas and trends. He was tall and dark-haired, with a particularly broad build. His red face had an air of self-satisfaction, and his teeth were as white as sugar. He carried himself with a polished, gentlemanly manner and was known for being clever. In certain circles, people like him are often called clever. This label typically refers to a type of person who thrives at others' expense, contributes nothing, and has no intention of doing so. Their hearts seem hardened by a lifetime of laziness and idleness.

These men always have excuses, claiming they can't do anything because of complex and hostile circumstances that supposedly stand in their way. They like to talk about how their talents are wasted, saying things like, "It's tragic to see my abilities go unused." This phrase is their favorite excuse, their motto, one they repeat so often that it becomes tiresome and meaningless. Some of these characters, despite doing nothing, want everyone to believe that they are not shallow or selfish. They try to present themselves as having great depth, though even the best surgeon would find it hard to identify anything significant within them—out of politeness, of course.

These men succeed in life because they excel at sneering at others, criticizing their mistakes and weaknesses, and puffing themselves up with arrogance. Since they have no real emotional depth, it's easy for them to maintain their social position by exploiting others. They see themselves as masters of the world, convinced that everyone owes them something. To them, people are like oranges or sponges to squeeze for juice whenever needed, and they take great pride in this attitude. They see their success as a result of their supposed intelligence and character.

In their limitless arrogance, they refuse to see any flaws in themselves. They are like those clever con artists—such natural frauds that they genuinely believe their dishonesty is a form of virtue. They've told so many lies about their honesty that they've convinced even themselves that their deceitfulness is righteous. They lack the ability to reflect on their actions or to criticize themselves with any sincerity. They're simply too self-centered for that.

For men like him, their own egos are their gods, the only thing they worship. To them, the entire world is just a giant mirror created for their self-admiration. They look into it constantly, seeing only themselves, and ignoring everything else. It's no wonder they view the world so harshly. They always have a clever phrase ready for any situation, often the most fashionable or trendy line they can think of. In fact, they're the ones who help popularize these phrases, eagerly embracing ideas they think will make them look important.

They stockpile phrases about their supposed compassion for humanity, their opinions on philanthropy, and their attacks on anything "romantic." To them, anything romantic—anything fine or true—is worthless. They are too coarse to understand subtle truths or recognize value in ideas that are still developing or unfinished. Having spent their entire lives indulging in luxury, with everything provided for them, they have no understanding of hard work. And heaven help you if you offend their comfortable sensibilities. They'll never forgive you and will hold a grudge forever, waiting for an opportunity to get revenge.

In short, Madame M.'s husband was nothing more than a giant, bloated bag full of empty phrases, trendy ideas, and meaningless labels.

M. M., however, had a unique talent and was a remarkable man. He was witty, an excellent conversationalist, and a captivating storyteller, always drawing a crowd in any drawing room. That evening, he was particularly charming. He dominated the conversation, full of energy and clearly pleased about something, holding everyone's attention effortlessly. Meanwhile, Madame M. looked as though she were unwell. Her face was so sorrowful that I kept expecting tears to well up on her long eyelashes at any moment. All of this left a deep impression on me and filled me with wonder. I went to bed that night feeling strangely curious and dreamed about M. M., which was unusual for me, as I rarely ever dreamed.

The next morning, I was called to a rehearsal for some tableaux vivants in which I was to participate. These living pictures, along with a theatrical performance and a dance, were scheduled for five days later on the birthday of our host's younger daughter. Although the entertainment had been planned somewhat last-minute, another hundred guests were invited from Moscow and the surrounding villas, creating a flurry of excitement and activity. The rehearsal, or rather the costume fitting, was held early in the morning because the director—a well-known artist and a friend of our host—needed to leave for Moscow immediately to gather props and finalize preparations for the event. There wasn't a moment to waste. I was cast in a tableau with Madame M., a medieval scene titled "The Lady of the Castle and Her Page."

When I saw Madame M. at the rehearsal, I was overwhelmed with nervousness. I felt as though she could read all of my thoughts and suspicions from the day before just by looking into my eyes. I also couldn't shake the feeling that I had done something wrong by stumbling upon her tears the previous day and interrupting her grief. I worried she might see me as an unwelcome witness to her sadness, someone she couldn't forgive for sharing her secret. Fortunately, it all went smoothly; in fact, I wasn't noticed at all. It seemed she had no attention to spare for me or the rehearsal.

She appeared distracted, sorrowful, and lost in deep thought, clearly weighed down by some great concern.

As soon as my part was finished, I quickly changed out of my costume and went out onto the verandah and into the garden. At almost the same moment, Madame M. came outside through another door. Not long after, her self-satisfied husband appeared, returning from the garden where he had just escorted a group of ladies and handed them over to a capable companion.

The meeting between the husband and wife seemed unplanned. Madame M. suddenly looked flustered, and there was a faint trace of irritation in the way she moved. Her husband, who had been carelessly whistling a tune while stroking his whiskers with exaggerated seriousness, stopped when he saw her. He frowned slightly and gave her a piercing, scrutinizing look, almost as though he were interrogating her without words.

"You're going into the garden?" he asked, noticing the parasol and book in her hand.

"No, into the woods," she said, with a faint blush.

"Alone?"

"With him," said Madame M., pointing at me. "I always take a walk alone in the morning," she added in an uncertain, hesitant voice, the way people speak when they tell their first lie.

"Hmm... and I've just taken the whole group there. They're all gathered in the flower arbor to say goodbye to N. He's leaving, you know... Something's gone wrong in Odessa. Your cousin"—he meant the fair-haired beauty—"is laughing and crying at the same time; she's impossible to figure out. But she says you're angry with N. about something and that's why you wouldn't come to see him off. That's nonsense, right?"

"She's laughing," said Madame M., descending the steps of the verandah.

"So this is your daily cavaliere servente," M. M. added with a sarcastic smile, lifting his lorgnette to look at me.

"Page!" I snapped, annoyed by his lorgnette and his mocking tone. Laughing in his face, I jumped down the three verandah steps in one leap.

"Enjoy your walk," muttered M. M. as he went on his way.

Naturally, I joined Madame M. immediately after she gestured to her husband that I was coming with her. I acted as if she had invited me to walk with her hours ago and as if I had been her regular walking companion every morning for the past month. But I couldn't understand why she seemed so uneasy and embarrassed or why she had resorted to that little lie. Why hadn't she simply said she was going alone? I didn't know how to look at her, but I couldn't help being amazed. Bit by bit, I began glancing shyly at her face, as though trying to read her thoughts. Yet, just like earlier during the rehearsal, she didn't notice my silent questions or my gaze.

Her expression showed the same anxiety, but it was now more intense and obvious. Her unease was evident in her hurried walk and in the way she kept glancing nervously down every path leading toward the garden. She quickened her pace more and more, her eyes scanning every avenue and trail. It felt as though she were waiting for something—or someone. I found myself feeling the same anticipation.

Suddenly, we heard the sound of horses' hooves behind us. It was the group of ladies and gentlemen on horseback, escorting N., the man who was abruptly leaving our company.

Among the ladies was my fair tormentor, the one M. M. had mentioned as being in tears. True to her character, however, she was laughing like a carefree child and galloping confidently on a magnificent bay horse. When they reached us, N. tipped his hat but didn't stop or say a single word to Madame M. Soon, the entire group of riders disappeared from view.

I glanced at Madame M. and was nearly overcome with shock. She was standing as pale as a sheet, and large tears were streaming down her face. By chance, our eyes met. Madame M. quickly flushed, turned away, and for a moment, a look of discomfort and frustration crossed her face. I could tell more clearly than ever that I was in the way—worse than before. But how could I leave without it being awkward?

As if sensing my dilemma, Madame M. opened the book in her hand. Blushing and clearly avoiding my gaze, she said, as though she had just realized it, "Ah! This is the second part. I've made a mistake. Please bring me the first."

Her meaning was unmistakable. My role in this moment was done, and I couldn't have been more clearly dismissed.

I ran off with her book and didn't return. The first part of the book sat untouched on the table for the rest of the morning.

But I couldn't shake a strange feeling of unease. My heart was filled with an odd, haunting anxiety. I avoided crossing paths with Madame M. as much as I could, but

I couldn't help staring at the smug figure of M. M. with a wild curiosity, as though there had to be something extraordinary about him. I didn't understand why I felt this absurd fascination. All I knew was that I was deeply unsettled by everything I had seen that morning.

And yet, the day was far from over, and it would bring even more unexpected events for me.

Dinner was served very early that day because an outing to a nearby village festival had been planned for the evening, and everyone needed time to prepare. I had been dreaming about this excursion for the past three days, imagining all sorts of exciting things. After dinner, most of the group gathered on the verandah for coffee. I followed cautiously, keeping myself hidden behind the third row of chairs. I was curious about what was happening but didn't want Madame M. to notice me.

Unfortunately, I found myself not far from my fair tormentor. Something extraordinary seemed to be happening with her that day—she looked twice as beautiful as usual. I don't know how or why this happens, but such transformations in women are not uncommon. Among us was a new guest, a tall, pale-faced young man who had just arrived from Moscow. He was the official admirer of our fair beauty, seemingly there to take the place of N., who, according to rumors, had been madly in love with her. This new admirer had a relationship with her reminiscent of Benedick and Beatrice in Shakespeare's Much Ado About Nothing.

The fair beauty was at her absolute best that day. Her cheerful chatter and playful jokes were charming and lighthearted. She was so confident in her ability to captivate everyone that she naturally became the center of attention. A crowd of amazed and admiring listeners surrounded her constantly, and she had never seemed so enchanting. Every word she spoke was captivating and clever, passed eagerly from one listener to another. Not a single joke, remark, or playful comment was missed. It seemed no one had expected her to display such wit and elegance. Usually, her good qualities were buried under her wild and impulsive behavior—playful antics that often bordered on childish mischief. Because of this, her brilliance was rarely noticed, and when it was, it was met with skepticism. Now, however, her sparkling wit left everyone whispering in amazement.

There was, however, one unusual and somewhat sensitive aspect of the situation. Madame M.'s husband played an unexpected role in the fair beauty's success. The lively woman boldly launched an attack on him— an assault that, to the amusement of almost everyone, especially the younger people, was welcomed with delight. She peppered him with a series of witty remarks, mockery, and sarcasm. Her teasing was so skillfully disguised in polite language that it hit its mark without giving him anything to directly respond to. Her comments left him flustered and exhausted, his efforts to counter her completely futile. The more he tried to defend himself, the more he was reduced to frustrated, almost comical despair.

I couldn't say for sure, but I suspect her entire performance had been planned in advance. This verbal duel had actually begun earlier during dinner. I call it a duel because it truly was fierce. Madame M.'s husband was not one to give up easily. He summoned all his wit and quick thinking in an effort to avoid being completely humiliated. Throughout their exchange, the room was filled with endless laughter from everyone watching and listening.

For him, this day was nothing like the one before. Several times, I noticed Madame M. trying to stop her bold friend from going too far. It was clear that the fair beauty was intentionally trying to portray her husband as an absurdly jealous man, possibly even a "bluebeard" figure. This impression stayed with me, especially given how events unfolded later and the role I eventually played in the matter.

I got dragged into the whole situation in the most ridiculous way, completely by surprise. At the worst possible moment, I was standing right where everyone could see me, completely unaware of what was coming and forgetting all the precautions I had so carefully practiced for so long. All of a sudden, I was thrust into the spotlight as if I were a sworn enemy and natural rival of M. M., accused of being desperately in love with his wife. My tormentor, with complete confidence, swore that she had proof and even claimed that just that morning she had seen something in the woods...

But before she could finish, I jumped in at the most desperate moment. That moment had been so devilishly planned, so carefully set up for its ridiculous finale, and delivered with such sharp humor that the entire room erupted in uncontrollable laughter at her final jab. Even though I could sense that my part in this spectacle wasn't the worst, I was so overwhelmed—confused, irritated, and panicked—that, completely miserable and on the verge of tears, I pushed my way through two rows of chairs. I stepped forward, and, addressing my tormentor with a voice shaking from both tears and outrage, I cried out:

"Aren't you ashamed... to say such a terrible lie... in front of all these ladies... out loud? Like a little child... in front of everyone here. What will they think? A grown woman like you... and married!"

But I couldn't finish. The room exploded into a deafening roar of laughter and applause. My outburst caused such a sensation that even now, when I remember it, I can't help but laugh at the absurdity of it all. My naïve protest, my tears, and especially the way it seemed like I was defending M. M.—all of it was so unexpected and ridiculous that it sent everyone into fits of laughter.

I was completely humiliated, overwhelmed by confusion and shame. Burning with embarrassment, I covered my face with my hands and ran out of the room. In my haste, I bumped into a footman at the door and sent the tray he was carrying crashing to the floor. Without stopping, I bolted upstairs to my room, yanked the key from the outside of the door, and locked myself in. It was the right decision because, within moments, a group of the prettiest ladies in the house had gathered outside my door.

I could hear their ringing laughter, their cheerful voices, and their endless chatter. They all started calling to me at once, their excited voices overlapping like a flock of swallows. They begged me to open the door, even for just a moment. They promised no harm would come to me and claimed they only wanted to shower me with kisses.

But what could have been more horrifying than such a strange and embarrassing threat? I buried my face in the pillows, burning with shame, and didn't open the door or even answer them. The ladies kept knocking for a long time, but I stayed silent and stubborn, as only an eleven-year-old boy can be.

But what could I do now? Everything had been exposed, everything I had tried so hard to hide and protect! I felt like everlasting disgrace and shame had fallen on me. Yet, the truth was, I couldn't even explain why I was so afraid or what exactly I wanted to keep hidden. Still, I was terrified of something and had trembled at the thought of it being discovered. Until that moment, I hadn't even known what "it" was— whether it was something good or bad, admirable or embarrassing. Now, in the middle of my misery, I felt certain that it was ridiculous and shameful.

At the same time, deep down, I instinctively knew this judgment was wrong, cruel, and unfair. But I was crushed, completely overwhelmed. My thoughts were scattered, and I couldn't make sense of anything. I wasn't able to fight back against this harsh verdict or question it. I was confused, and all I could feel was that my heart had been deeply and shamelessly hurt. Tears filled my eyes, and I felt powerless. I was angry—burning with a fury and hatred I had never felt before. For the first time in my life, I truly understood what it was to feel insulted, hurt, and sorrowful. And it was no small thing.

My first unformed feelings had been roughly trampled on, as if they didn't matter. My first innocent, delicate sense of modesty had been exposed and insulted, and perhaps my first real, beautiful impression of something pure had been mocked. Of course, my tormentors didn't fully understand what I was going through or even guess at the depth of my pain. There was one part of it—something I hadn't been able to understand or analyze until then—that I had feared and avoided thinking about.

I stayed on my bed in despair, burying my face in the pillow, torn between feeling feverish and freezing. Two questions tormented me. First, what exactly had the fair tormentor seen that morning in the woods? What could she have possibly noticed between Madame M. and me? And second, how could I ever look Madame M. in the face again without dying of shame and despair?

A sudden noise in the yard broke me out of my half-conscious state. I sat up and went to the window. The yard was crowded with carriages, saddled horses, and bustling servants. It looked like everyone was preparing to leave. Some of the gentlemen were already on their horses, and others were climbing into the carriages.

Then I remembered the planned trip to the village festival. A feeling of unease crept over me as I began searching for my pony in the yard. But I didn't see it anywhere. That must mean they had forgotten about me. Unable to stop myself, I rushed downstairs, completely forgetting about the awkward encounters or the shame I had been drowning in just moments before.

Terrible news awaited me. There was no horse or seat available in any of the carriages for me. Everything had been arranged, all the seats were taken, and I had to make way for others. Crushed by this new disappointment, I stood on the steps, staring sadly at the long rows of coaches, carriages, and chaises. There wasn't even the smallest space left for me. I looked at the elegantly dressed ladies, whose restless horses pranced and shifted on the spot.

One of the gentlemen was running late, and everyone was waiting for him to arrive so they could set off. His horse stood at the door, chewing on the bit, pawing at the ground with its hooves, and occasionally rearing up. Two stable boys held the horse firmly by the bridle, but everyone else kept a safe distance, watching cautiously.

A frustrating situation had caused my exclusion. Not only had new visitors arrived, taking up all the seats, but two of the horses had fallen ill—one of them being my pony. I wasn't the only one affected, though. It turned out that there wasn't a horse available for the new guest, the pale-faced young man I had mentioned earlier. To solve this, our host had to take the extreme step of offering his wild, unbroken stallion. He warned the guest, adding that the horse was impossible to ride and that they had been planning to sell it for its dangerous nature if they could find a buyer.

Despite the warning, the young man confidently declared that he was a skilled horseman and would ride anything rather than miss the trip. Our host said nothing more, but I thought I noticed a sly, ambiguous smile playing on his lips. He waited patiently for the confident guest to appear, rubbing his hands together and glancing at the door with an expression of anticipation. The two stable boys, holding the fiery stallion, seemed to share a similar feeling. They stood proudly, almost bursting with excitement at being in charge of a horse that could potentially harm or even kill someone at any moment. Their eyes, round with expectation, stayed fixed on the door, waiting for the daring young man to arrive.

The horse itself acted as though it was part of this strange conspiracy with the host and the stable boys. It carried itself with pride and arrogance, seeming fully aware that dozens of curious eyes were watching it. It seemed to bask in its wicked reputation, much like an infamous criminal reveling in stories of their misdeeds. The stallion's posture dared anyone bold enough to try and tame its wild spirit, as if mocking the brave soul who thought they could control it.

The bold young man finally appeared. Looking guilty for keeping everyone waiting, he hurriedly pulled on his gloves as he came forward, not glancing at anything around him. He ran down the steps and only looked up as he reached out to grab the mane of the waiting horse. But the horse's wild rearing, combined with a frightened scream from the onlookers, made him hesitate. He stepped back, staring in confusion at the vicious animal. The horse was trembling with rage, snorting angrily, and rolling its bloodshot eyes. It kept rearing up on its hind legs, thrashing its forelegs in the air as if it might bolt into the sky, dragging the two stable boys holding it along for the ride.

For a moment, the young man stood frozen, clearly unsure of what to do. Then, with a faint blush of embarrassment, he looked up at the nervous ladies watching him.

"A very fine horse!" he said, almost to himself. "And I'd imagine it would be quite thrilling to ride him. But… you know, I think I won't go," he added, turning to our host with a broad, good-natured smile that matched his kind and intelligent expression.

"Well, I must say, I think you're an excellent horseman, truly," replied the host, clearly pleased. He shook the young man's hand warmly, almost as if he were thanking him. "And that's because, from the very first moment, you understood what kind of beast you were dealing with," he added with an air of authority. "Would you believe it, even though I served twenty-three years in the hussars, I've had the pleasure of being thrown to the ground three times by that animal—every single time I tried to ride him. Tancred, my boy, there's no one here who's a match for you! It seems your rider must be some legendary Ilya Muromets, and he's probably sitting quietly in the village of Kapatcharovo, waiting for your teeth to fall out. Come, take him away; he's scared enough people already. It was a waste of time bringing him out," the host said, rubbing his hands with satisfaction.

It should be noted that Tancred was utterly useless to his owner and did nothing but eat corn for free. On top of that, the old hussar had damaged his reputation as a judge of horses by paying an outrageous amount for this beast—purchasing him solely for his looks. Yet, at this moment, the host seemed delighted that Tancred had lived up to his wild reputation, defeated yet another potential rider, and earned himself another round of meaningless glory.

"So, you're not going?" cried the blonde beauty, clearly annoyed that her escort might not be joining the trip. "Surely you're not scared?"

"Honestly, I am," replied the young man.

"Are you serious?"

"Do you want me to break my neck?" he said with a shrug.

"Then hurry up and take my horse! Don't worry, it's very gentle. We won't hold anyone up—they can switch the saddles in no time! I'll try riding yours. Tancred can't always be so difficult, can he?"

No sooner had she spoken than she jumped off her horse and stood before us, finishing her sentence as she did so.

"You clearly don't know Tancred if you think he'll allow your flimsy side-saddle to be strapped onto him!" our host exclaimed. "Besides, I wouldn't want you to break your neck—it'd be a shame!" As he spoke, he adopted his usual tone of gruffness and bluntness, something he often used to appear like a cheerful, rough-and-ready old soldier. He believed this act made him especially appealing to women. It was one of his little habits, something we all knew well.

"Well, crybaby, don't you want to give it a try? You were so eager to come along, weren't you?" said the daring horsewoman, noticing me and pointing mockingly at Tancred. I had been foolish enough to meet her gaze, and she wasn't about to let me escape without a sharp remark. It seemed she didn't want to have dismounted her horse for nothing.

"I'm sure you're not such a coward—we all know you're a hero and would be too proud to back down. Especially when people are watching you, brave little page," she added with a quick glance at Madame M., whose carriage was parked closest to the entrance.

A surge of hatred and a thirst for revenge filled my heart when the daring Amazon approached us, intending to mount Tancred. I can't put into words what I felt when she suddenly challenged me like that.

Everything went dark before my eyes as I saw her glance at Madame M. For a split second, an idea flashed through my mind—just for a moment, less than a moment, like the spark of gunpowder. Maybe it was the final straw. Suddenly, my anger boiled over, and my spirit surged with a fiery determination. I wanted to put all my enemies to shame and take revenge on everyone, right there, in front of them all, by proving who I truly was.

Or perhaps it wasn't that at all. Maybe some wild, romantic image from medieval tales—stories I hadn't even read yet—swept through my dizzy brain. Visions of tournaments, knights, brave heroes, beautiful ladies, the clash of swords, cheers from the crowd, and, within those shouts, the timid cry of a frightened heart. Somehow, that seemed more moving than any victory or fame. I don't know if all that romantic nonsense was in my mind at that moment, or if it was just the beginning of the foolishness that would later become a part of me. Whatever it was, I felt like my moment had come. My heart pounded and trembled, and before I knew what was happening, I had jumped down the steps and stood beside Tancred.

"You think I'm afraid?" I shouted, boldly and proudly. I was so overwhelmed with excitement that my vision blurred, my breath came in gasps, and my cheeks burned with the heat of tears. "I'll show you!" I cried. Grabbing hold of Tancred's mane, I put my foot in the stirrup before anyone could stop me. But at that exact moment, Tancred reared up, threw his head back, and with a powerful leap forward, tore free from the stunned stable boys. Like a hurricane, he bolted, and the crowd cried out in horror.

I have no idea how I managed to swing my other leg over the horse while it was galloping full speed. I don't know how I kept hold of the reins either. Tancred raced past the trellis gate, turned sharply to the right, and charged forward along the fence, ignoring the path altogether. It was only then that I heard the shouts of fifty voices behind me. That sound echoed in my heart, filling it with a strange mix of pride and joy that I will never forget. In that wild moment of my boyhood, all the blood rushed to my head, overpowering my fear and making me feel almost invincible.

Looking back now, I can't help but think there was something knightly, something of a wandering hero, in that reckless act.

My knightly adventures, however, were over almost as quickly as they began—or things could have ended very badly for this so-called knight. Even now, I'm not entirely sure how I managed to escape unharmed. I did know how to ride, having been taught, but my experience was limited to a gentle pony that was more like a sheep than a horse. If Tancred had had more time to react, I have no doubt I would have been thrown off. After galloping for about fifty paces, he suddenly took fright at a large stone lying across the road. Without warning, he spun around sharply and bolted back the way we had come.

The speed and force of his turn were so violent that, even now, I can't understand how I wasn't flung from the saddle like a ball flying through the air. It's a wonder I wasn't sent twenty feet away, dashed to pieces on the ground, or that Tancred didn't injure himself with such an abrupt maneuver. He charged back toward the gate at full speed, tossing his head wildly, leaping from side to side like a creature drunk with rage. His powerful legs flailed randomly in the air as he tried with every bound to shake me off his back, as though I were some tiger clinging to him with sharp teeth and claws.

For a moment, I felt myself slipping and knew that I was about to be thrown. I was falling—there was no question of it—but at that critical moment, several gentlemen rushed to my rescue. Two of them quickly blocked Tancred's way before he could escape into the open fields. Meanwhile, two others galloped up beside him, closing in so tightly that their horses' sides pressed against my legs. They managed to grab Tancred by the bridle, bringing him to a stop.

A few seconds later, I was back at the steps, trembling as they lifted me down from the horse. My face was pale, and I could barely breathe. I shook like a blade of grass swaying in the wind. Tancred, too, was visibly shaken. His hooves were planted firmly into the ground as though he were bracing himself, his entire body leaning backward. His fiery breaths came in heavy puffs from his red, flared nostrils. He twitched and quivered all over, his pride and anger seemingly wounded by the idea that a mere child had dared to ride him and somehow survived.

All around me, voices rose in a chorus of astonishment, concern, and surprise. I could hear exclamations of bewilderment from every side. At that moment, my wandering gaze caught the eyes of Madame M., who was watching from nearby. She looked pale and visibly shaken. I will never forget what happened next. The instant our eyes met, my face burned as though it had been set on fire. A wave of heat rushed over me, and I turned scarlet. I don't know what came over me, but I was suddenly overwhelmed by my own emotions. Confused and frightened by what I was feeling, I quickly lowered my eyes to the ground.

But my glance had not gone unnoticed. It was caught—stolen, even—and immediately, all eyes turned toward Madame M. Finding herself suddenly at the center of attention, she flushed deeply, like a child caught in an unguarded moment. She tried to laugh it off, but the effort was awkward and did nothing to hide her embarrassment.

The entire situation must have seemed absurd from the outside, but something unexpected happened that saved me from the laughter of the crowd and completely changed the mood of the scene. The blonde beauty, who had been the instigator of the whole escapade and my relentless tormentor until now, suddenly rushed forward to embrace me. Her expression had completely changed. At first, she had barely believed her eyes when I accepted her challenge, daring to ride Tancred. She had been terrified and full of self-reproach when I bolted off on the wild horse. But now, as everything unfolded, and particularly after catching the look I had exchanged with Madame M.— my confusion and sudden blush—something about the moment stirred her.

The romantic, playful side of her nature took over, and her excitement reached its peak. Moved by an unexpected wave of enthusiasm for my "knightly" behavior, she approached me with a mix of joy, pride, and emotion. Throwing her arms around me, she pressed me to her chest. Her normally mischievous face took on a look of serious tenderness. Crystal tears shimmered in her eyes, betraying an emotion no one expected from someone so carefree. Turning to the crowd, she pointed at me and said in a steady, sincere voice, "Mais c'est très sérieux, messieurs, ne riez pas!" ("This is very serious, gentlemen, do not laugh!")

She didn't seem to realize that her sudden earnestness and the bright, fiery glow of her enthusiasm had captivated everyone around her. For a moment, the crowd stood in stunned silence, mesmerized by her words, her gestures, and the rare emotion in her tear-filled eyes. Her passion was so unexpected, so raw and genuine, that no one could look away. Even our host, known for his boisterous demeanor, flushed as red as a tulip. Later, some claimed to have heard him admit, "To my shame, I was in love with her for a whole minute."

In the end, after everything that had happened, I was no longer just a boy. I was a knight—a hero in their eyes.

"De Lorge! Toggenburg!" someone in the crowd shouted.

Applause broke out, and the cheers grew louder.

"Hurrah for the rising generation!" added the host with a booming laugh.

"But he has to come with us, he absolutely must come with us," said the blonde beauty, her voice brimming with excitement. "We'll find a place for him, we have to find a place! He can sit beside me—on my knee... oh no, wait, no, that's not right!" She burst into laughter, unable to contain her amusement at the memory of our earlier encounter. Even as she laughed, she reached out and stroked my hand gently, her touch soft and reassuring, as though trying to soothe me and ensure I wouldn't take offense at her playful teasing.

"Of course, of course, he must go! He's earned his place," several voices joined in eagerly, their agreement sealing the matter almost instantly.

The decision was made in no time. The older woman, the same one who had unwittingly introduced me to the blonde beauty, was surrounded by pleas from the younger group to give up her seat and stay behind so I could go in her place. Begrudgingly, and with barely concealed annoyance, she gave in. Though she smiled outwardly, her irritation slipped through in a quiet, angry hiss. Meanwhile, her usual defender—now my newfound ally—called out cheerfully as she rode off on her lively horse, laughing like a carefree child. "I envy you!" she said with mock regret. "I wish I could stay home myself. It's about to rain, and we're all going to get drenched!"

Her prediction came true. Within the hour, a heavy downpour soaked everything, bringing our excursion to a halt. We had no choice but to seek refuge in the small huts of the village, where we waited out the rain for hours. It wasn't until well after nine o'clock in the evening, under the damp mist left behind by the storm, that we finally returned home. By then, I was starting to feel feverish.

Just as we were preparing to leave the village, Madame M. approached me. She seemed surprised that my neck was exposed and that I wasn't wearing anything warm over my jacket. When I explained that I hadn't had time to grab a coat, she quickly took a pin and fastened the collar of my shirt to cover my neck. Without hesitation, she removed a crimson gauze scarf from around her own neck and wrapped it snugly around mine to keep me from catching a cold. She moved so quickly and matter-of-factly that I barely had time to process what was happening, let alone thank her.

When we finally returned home, I found Madame M. sitting in the small drawing room with the blonde beauty and the pale-faced young man, who had gained a reputation that day by cleverly avoiding the challenge of riding Tancred. Summoning my courage, I walked over to thank her and return the scarf. But now, after all the day's adventures, I felt oddly self-conscious. My face flushed with embarrassment, as it always seemed to, and I hurriedly handed back the scarf, eager to retreat upstairs where I could reflect in peace on everything that had happened.

"I bet he'd rather keep the scarf," the young man teased with a knowing laugh. "It's obvious he's reluctant to part with it."

"Exactly! That's it!" chimed in the blonde beauty. "What a boy!" She shook her head in mock frustration, clearly about to say something more but stopping herself when Madame M. gave her a serious, warning glance. Not wanting to push the joke too far, she fell silent.

Seizing the chance, I quickly excused myself and began to slip away.

"Wait a minute, you silly boy!" called the blonde beauty, catching up to me in the next room. She took my hands warmly, her tone playful yet affectionate. "If you wanted to keep the scarf so badly, why didn't you just say so? All you had to do was say you misplaced it, and that would've been the end of it. What a simpleton!

You can't even manage that! Oh, what a funny boy you are!"

As she laughed, she reached out and tapped my chin with her finger, her teasing lighthearted but unmistakable. My cheeks flushed bright red, as they always did, which only made her laugh harder. To her, my embarrassment seemed to be the most amusing part of all.

"I am your friend now, you know; am I not? Our enmity is over, isn't it? Yes or no?" she asked, her tone playful but earnest.

I laughed softly and squeezed her fingers in reply, saying nothing.

"Oh, but why are you so pale? Why are you shivering? Have you caught a chill?" she asked, leaning closer with genuine concern.

"Yes, I don't feel well," I admitted quietly.

"Ah, poor boy! That's what comes from too much excitement. Do you know what? You should go straight to bed and skip supper. You'll feel much better in the morning. Come on, let me help you."

She led me upstairs herself, her voice and manner full of warmth and care. Once we reached my room, she insisted I get ready for bed while she hurried back downstairs. A short while later, she returned with a cup of tea, bringing it to me herself as I lay under the covers. Not stopping there, she went back down again and brought up a warm quilt to make sure I was as comfortable as possible. Her kindness and attention left me deeply moved. Perhaps it was the strain of the day, the feverish haze I was in, or simply the gentleness of her actions, but I felt overwhelmed with gratitude.

When I said goodnight, I hugged her tightly, as though she were my closest and dearest friend. In my tired and emotional state, all the feelings and events of the day came rushing back to me in a wave. I felt tears welling up as I rested my head against her shoulder. She noticed my overwrought condition and, to my surprise, seemed touched by it herself.

"You're a very good boy," she said softly, looking at me with kind, gentle eyes. "Please don't be angry with me. You won't be, will you?"

From that moment, we became the best of friends—true, warm, and unshakable.

The next morning, I woke up quite early, but the sun was already flooding the room with its bright, golden light. I jumped out of bed feeling completely refreshed, as if I had never been ill the day before. In fact, I felt an unexplainable joy, a lightness of spirit that filled me with energy. Remembering the events of the previous day, I felt a strong longing to see my newfound friend again, the fair-haired beauty. I wished I could embrace her as warmly as I had the night before, but it was still too early and everyone else was asleep.

I dressed quickly and slipped out of the house into the garden. From there, I wandered into the copse, heading toward the densest part of the woods where the trees grew thickest and the air was filled with the rich, resinous scent of pine. The sunlight filtered through the branches, playfully breaking through the heavy shadows of the foliage, and the morning felt alive with its warmth and brightness. It was a perfect start to the day.

As I wandered further into the woods, I suddenly found myself at its edge, where the Moskva River flowed peacefully below. It lay about two hundred paces down the hill, and on the opposite bank, men were mowing the fields. I stood there for a while, watching the sharp blades of their scythes flash in the sunlight as they swung in unison. The cut grass flew to the side in rich, heavy swathes, falling into long, neat rows. I don't know how long I stood there, lost in thought, captivated by the scene.

My daydream was interrupted by the sound of a horse snorting and pawing the ground impatiently nearby. It seemed to be on the path that connected the main road to the manor house, about twenty paces from where I stood. I wasn't sure whether I had just heard it arrive or if the sound had been there for a while, blending into the background of my thoughts. Curiosity got the better of me, and I stepped back into the cover of the woods, moving carefully toward the noise.

As I crept closer, I began to hear voices speaking quickly but in hushed tones. Parting the branches gently, I peered through the bushes lining the path, and what I saw made me leap back in astonishment. I caught sight of a familiar white dress, and the soft, melodic voice that reached my ears sent a thrill through my heart. It was Madame M. She stood beside a man on horseback, who was leaning down from the saddle, speaking to her in hurried tones. To my amazement, I recognized him—it was N., the young man who had left the day before, causing such a commotion with his departure.

I stared in disbelief. Everyone had said he was going far away, to the southern regions of Russia, and yet here he was, back already, standing alone with Madame M. in the quiet of the woods.

The young man was holding her hand, leaning down to kiss it with what appeared to be a blend of urgency and tenderness. I had stumbled upon them at the very moment of parting, and it was clear that time was pressing. After what seemed like a lingering hesitation, he reached into his pocket and pulled out a sealed envelope, placing it firmly in Madame M.'s hand. Without dismounting from his horse, he wrapped one arm around her and pressed a long, fervent kiss to her lips. It was the kind of kiss that spoke of finality, of unspoken emotions that could no longer be contained. A moment later, he whipped the reins, and his horse bolted away, carrying him past me like an arrow shot from a bow.

Madame M. stood watching him as he disappeared, her gaze following him until he was out of sight. For a few moments, she seemed frozen, as though rooted to the spot, lost in thought. Then, with a sigh that seemed to carry the weight of her sorrow, she turned and began walking back toward the house. Her steps were slow and heavy, reflecting the sadness in her posture. But after taking only a few steps along the narrow track, she seemed to suddenly remember something. With a start, she hurriedly parted the bushes and disappeared into the copse.

I followed her, though I wasn't sure why. My heart was pounding violently, as though something terrifying lay ahead. I was overwhelmed, not just by what I had seen but by the torrent of emotions it stirred within me.

I felt as if my thoughts had been scattered to the wind, leaving me dazed and uncertain. Sadness seemed to envelop me for reasons I couldn't fully explain. Through the gaps in the foliage, I caught glimpses of her white dress moving steadily ahead of me. I trailed after her without thinking, never letting her out of my sight, though the fear that she might notice me sent shivers down my spine.

Eventually, she emerged onto the small path that led back to the house. I paused for a moment, watching her disappear into the distance before stepping out of the bushes myself. But to my astonishment, lying there on the red sand of the path was a sealed packet—the very envelope I had just seen handed to her.

I bent down to pick it up, my heart pounding with a mix of curiosity and dread. The envelope was blank on both sides, with no address or markings of any kind. Though it wasn't very large, it felt thick and heavy, as if it contained several sheets of paper—perhaps three or more.

What could this envelope mean? I couldn't help but think it held the key to all the mysteries that had unfolded before my eyes. Perhaps it contained everything the young man hadn't been able to express during their brief, hurried parting. He hadn't even dismounted from his horse—was it because he was pressed for time, or because he feared his emotions might betray him if he lingered? I couldn't say.

I stood frozen, staring at the envelope in my hand. Then, feeling conflicted, I placed it back on the path in the most obvious spot I could find, hoping Madame M. would notice her loss and return to retrieve it. I watched the envelope intently, waiting, but after several agonizing minutes, there was no sign of her. Unable to bear the suspense any longer, I picked it up again, tucked it into my pocket, and set off to catch up with her.

I found her walking briskly along the wide garden avenue, heading straight for the house. Her steps were hurried, but her head was bowed, and her eyes were fixed on the ground as though she were lost in deep thought. I hesitated, unsure of what to do. Should I approach her and return the envelope? That would mean admitting I had seen everything. The moment I spoke, I would give myself away. How could I even face her? And how would she look at me?

I kept hoping she would realize the envelope was missing and retrace her steps. Then, I could discreetly toss it onto the path for her to find without ever knowing I'd been involved. But she didn't stop. She walked on, her pace quickening as we drew nearer to the house, where others had begun to stir.

As fate would have it, everyone had risen early that morning, likely to make plans after the previous evening's failed expedition. Breakfast was being served on the verandah, and the air buzzed with excitement. Not wanting to draw attention to myself by walking in with her, I waited in the garden for ten minutes, taking a longer route to approach the house from the other side. By the time I arrived, Madame M. was pacing back and forth on the verandah, her arms folded tightly across her chest. Her face was pale, and her agitation was evident in every step she took. She seemed to be making a tremendous effort to maintain her composure, but the despair in her eyes was unmistakable.

Occasionally, she would step down from the verandah and wander a few paces toward the flower beds or along the sandy path leading to the garden. Her eyes darted about impatiently, scanning the ground with a restless, almost frantic energy. It was clear she had discovered her loss and was convinced she had dropped the letter somewhere near the house. There was no doubt in my mind—she was searching for the envelope.Someone noticed that she was unusually pale and agitated, and soon others began to comment as well. Concerned voices surrounded her, asking after her health and offering sympathetic remarks. She had no choice but to put on a brave face. She laughed lightly, made a few playful remarks, and tried her best to appear lively, but her discomfort was unmistakable. From time to time, she glanced toward her husband, who stood at the far end of the terrace engaged in conversation with two ladies. Each time her eyes fell on him, she seemed to tremble slightly, overcome by the same unease and embarrassment she had shown the day he first arrived.

Meanwhile, I stood a little apart from the group, my hand thrust deep into my pocket, clutching the letter tightly. My heart ached for her, and I silently willed her to notice me. I wanted nothing more than to comfort her, to ease her obvious anxiety, if only with a quick glance or a whispered word. Yet when her gaze did eventually meet mine, I panicked and immediately looked away, unable to hold her eyes.

I could see how tormented she was, and I wasn't mistaken in my judgment. To this day, I don't know the full truth of her secret. All I have is what I saw and what I've just described. Perhaps the situation wasn't as it might have seemed at first glance. Perhaps that kiss was a farewell, a final gesture marking the end of something significant. Perhaps it was a small, bittersweet reward for a sacrifice made in the name of her peace and honor. N. was leaving her, perhaps forever. Even the letter I was holding tightly in my hand—who could say what it contained? Who could truly understand its meaning or the emotions it carried? And who had the right to judge?

Yet one thing was certain: the sudden revelation of her secret would have been catastrophic. It would have been a devastating blow, one from which she might never recover. I still remember her face at that moment. It was etched with such deep suffering that it seemed to bear the weight of an impending disaster. To know, to feel, to anticipate, with unshakable certainty, that at any moment—within the hour, the next quarter, or even the next few minutes—the truth might be exposed must have been unbearable. The letter could be found by someone else, picked up, opened. It bore no address, and its contents might be read by prying eyes. And then... what? What unspeakable torment awaited her in that eventuality?

I imagined the anguish she must have felt, standing among those who would become her judges if the truth came to light. The same faces that now offered her smiles and kind words would, in an instant, turn cold and merciless. She would see mockery, scorn, and unrelenting contempt in their expressions. Her life, as she knew it, would be over, plunged into an unending darkness from which there would be no escape. At the time, I couldn't fully comprehend this as I do now. All

I felt then was a vague sense of foreboding, an ache in my chest for the danger she faced, even if I didn't entirely understand it. Whatever her secret may have been, if it required atonement, her suffering in those moments surely counted for something. Her anguish was real, and I was a helpless witness to it.

Just as the tension seemed unbearable, a cheerful call to set off interrupted the heavy atmosphere. Almost immediately, the mood shifted. Everyone began bustling about, laughing and chatting with renewed energy. Within a matter of moments, the verandah emptied as the group prepared to leave. Madame M., however, declined to join the outing. Finally admitting that she wasn't feeling well, she excused herself. Thankfully, the lively preparations kept everyone too busy to linger or pester her with questions and advice.

Her husband approached her briefly to inquire after her health. She reassured him that she would be fine, that there was no need to worry, and that she didn't need to rest. She mentioned casually that she planned to take a walk in the garden—alone, except for me. At this, she glanced in my direction. The subtle acknowledgment made my heart leap with unexpected joy. A minute later, we set off together.

We walked along the same paths she had taken earlier that morning when returning from the copse. Her steps were quick but thoughtful, as though she was retracing her movements instinctively. Her gaze was fixed on the ground, scanning intently as though searching for something. She said nothing to me, perhaps forgetting I was there at all. It was as if her mind was far away, lost in a labyrinth of thoughts and emotions. All I could do was walk beside her in silence, feeling both her tension and my own as the weight of the unspoken hung heavily between us.

But just as we reached the spot where I had found the letter, where the path itself came to an end, Madame M. suddenly stopped. Her face was pale, her expression strained, and her voice was barely audible as she murmured that she felt worse and would return home. She took a few steps toward the garden fence but then paused again, standing still as if lost in thought. After a moment, a faint, bitter smile crossed her lips. It was a smile that spoke of despair and resignation, as though she had decided to face whatever consequences awaited her. Without a word, she turned back, retracing her steps, and seemed so consumed by her thoughts that she forgot to even mention her change of plans to me.

I was overwhelmed with sympathy, my heart aching for her, yet I felt completely powerless. I didn't know how to help or what to say to ease her obvious suffering. My mind raced as I followed her, trying to think of something—anything—that might bring her some small relief.

We found ourselves at the spot where, earlier that morning, I had overheard the sound of hoofbeats and caught fragments of their conversation. Beneath the cool shade of a sprawling elm tree was a stone bench, hewn from a single massive boulder and surrounded by ivy, wild jasmine, and dog-roses. The entire wood was dotted with similar charming surprises—small bridges, cozy arbors, and picturesque grottoes designed to delight any passerby. Madame M. sat down heavily on the stone bench, her movements mechanical, as though she were being propelled by sheer habit rather than any conscious intention. She glanced absently at the breathtaking view that stretched out before us, her eyes skimming over the scene without truly seeing it.

A minute later, she opened the book she had been carrying, holding it as if to read, but her gaze remained fixed on a single page. She did not turn the pages, nor did she seem to register the words. She sat there, lost in a fog of grief, completely detached from the beauty around her.

It was nearly half-past nine. The sun, high in the clear, dark blue sky, glowed brilliantly, its light spreading like molten gold. Across the river, the mowers were far away now, their figures barely visible from where we sat. Behind them stretched endless ridges of freshly cut grass, lying in neat rows. Every now and then, the soft breeze carried the fragrant aroma of the mown hay to us, mingling with the scents of the wildflowers nearby. Above and around us, the air was alive with the gentle hum of insects and the flutter of wings. It felt as though every flower and blade of grass was offering its essence to the Creator, whispering silently, "Father, I am blessed and happy."

Yet amidst all this vibrant life, Madame M. seemed utterly lifeless, like a figure carved from stone. Her sorrow was a stark contrast to the joyous energy of the world around her. I glanced at her and saw two large tears clinging to her lashes, unmoving, as though too heavy to fall. They seemed to have been wrung from the depths of her heart, a testament to her silent anguish. My heart ached to help her, to say or do something that might bring her comfort. I felt as though I was on the verge of speaking a hundred times, but every time I tried, my face burned with embarrassment, and I lost my courage.

Then, suddenly, an idea struck me, simple yet bright, and it filled me with a renewed sense of purpose. This was the solution I had been searching for.

"Would you like me to pick you a bouquet of flowers?" I asked, my voice brimming with eagerness. It was such a simple question, but I couldn't help the joy that crept into my tone.

She looked up at me, startled, as though pulled from the depths of her despair. For a moment, she studied my face intently, then, in a soft and almost trembling voice, she replied, "Yes, do." A faint smile touched her lips before she lowered her gaze back to the book in her lap.

"Of course! I'll hurry before the mowers get to them, or there won't be any left," I said enthusiastically, already moving to begin my task.

I set to work with an energy I hadn't felt in hours, gathering a simple yet heartfelt bouquet. Though the flowers were plain, I took care in selecting each one. I started close to the bench, picking dog-roses and wild jasmine that grew nearby. Remembering a rye field not far off, I ran to collect cornflowers, which I mixed with the tall, golden ears of rye, choosing the finest stalks I could find. A little farther along, I stumbled upon a nest of delicate forget-me-nots, their tiny blue blossoms adding a gentle touch to the bouquet.

Venturing deeper into the meadow, I found clusters of deep-blue campanulas and bright wild pinks. Then, down by the riverbank, I spotted yellow water lilies floating gracefully on the surface. With some effort, I managed to pluck a few, their cheerful color adding warmth to the arrangement. Finally, I wandered into the woods, where I gathered bright green, fan-shaped maple leaves to frame the bouquet. To my delight, I stumbled across a family of pansies nearby. Their soft colors seemed to glow in the dappled sunlight, and just beyond them, the sweet fragrance of violets betrayed their hiding place in the thick grass, still glistening with dew.

When the bouquet was complete, I bound it carefully with long, supple blades of grass twisted into a rope. Then, with a quiet determination, I tucked the letter into the center of the flowers, concealing it just enough that it wouldn't be obvious at first glance but would easily catch her attention once noticed.

Holding the bouquet in my hands, I felt a deep sense of satisfaction, my heart lighter than it had been all morning. Slowly, I made my way back to Madame M., the nosegay ready to offer her not only beauty but a small moment of relief—and perhaps, hope.

As I carried the bouquet toward her, I couldn't help but feel a growing unease. The letter, nestled among the flowers, seemed far too visible. I slowed my pace, adjusting the blooms to obscure it a little more. Yet as I walked closer, the sense of exposure gnawed at me, and I pushed it further into the bouquet. Finally, just as I reached her, a wave of panic seized me, and I thrust the letter so deeply into the center of the flowers that it became completely hidden. My cheeks burned fiercely with embarrassment, and the urge to hide my face and flee nearly overwhelmed me.

She glanced at the bouquet briefly, her expression distant, as though she had forgotten entirely that I had gathered it. Mechanically, she extended her hand, taking the flowers almost absentmindedly. Without a word, she set them down on the bench beside her and returned her gaze to her book. Her detachment stung, and I stood there for a moment, rooted in disappointment. My carefully gathered bouquet, meant to carry so much meaning, now lay forgotten. My heart sank. If only she would pick it up again! If only she would notice!

Unable to bear the awkwardness, I retreated a short distance and lay down on the grass. Resting my head on my arm, I closed my eyes, feigning sleep. But my senses remained sharp, and my thoughts fixed on her every move. I could see her from the corner of my eye, her still figure framed by the bright sunlight filtering through the leaves. Minutes dragged on, each one feeling like an eternity. I thought she looked even paler, her face etched with a quiet sorrow that seemed only to deepen.

And then, unexpectedly, fate intervened. A large, golden bee, carried on the soft summer breeze, appeared as if sent by some unseen hand. It buzzed over my head, its low hum breaking the silence, and then circled toward her. At first, she waved it away absently, her motions half-hearted. But the bee persisted, its determination matching my own hidden hope. Finally, she picked up the bouquet and began using it to swat the intruder.

As she moved the flowers, the letter slipped free and fell directly onto the open pages of her book. Time seemed to stop. She froze, staring at the letter in disbelief. Her wide eyes shifted back and forth between the letter and the bouquet still in her hands, as though struggling to comprehend what had just happened. Slowly, color rose to her cheeks, and a look of shock gave way to one of realization. She turned her head suddenly, her gaze locking onto me.

Though I felt her eyes on me, I squeezed mine shut, pretending to be asleep. My body tensed, and I fought the urge to react. My heart thundered in my chest, pounding so loudly that I feared she might hear it. I concentrated on keeping my breathing steady, even as every muscle in my body betrayed my inner turmoil. I felt her presence near me, her warmth radiating in the space between us.

She didn't move for what felt like an eternity. Then, out of the corner of my mind's eye, I sensed her bending down toward me. Her breath, warm and uneven, brushed against my face, and I knew she was studying me closely, searching for some sign that I was awake. My eyelashes quivered despite my efforts to stay still. Then I felt it—a soft, trembling kiss pressed to my hand, accompanied by the warmth of her tears.

The sound of voices calling her name broke the spell. "Madame M.! Natalie! Natalie!" someone called from afar. She remained silent, motionless for a moment, as though unsure whether to respond.

The voices came closer. "Natalie! Where are you?"

This time she spoke, her voice low and trembling, so quiet that only I could hear. "Coming," she said softly, her tone choked with emotion.

She bent closer still, and in that instant, her lips brushed against mine in a kiss that burned like fire. The suddenness of it sent a shock through me, and I let out a faint cry. My eyes flew open, but before I could fully register what had happened, she placed the soft crimson scarf over my face, as though shielding me from the sun—or from the world. The touch of the gauze was gentle, but the moment was fleeting.

Then, as quickly as she had come, she was gone. I heard the hurried sound of her retreating steps as they grew fainter and fainter. I was left lying there, the world around me hushed, as though holding its breath. I was alone, but the memory of her touch lingered, etched into my heart forever.

I took her scarf and kissed it, overcome with a surge of joy that I could barely contain. For several moments, I felt as though I had lost myself completely, overwhelmed by the intensity of my emotions. Breathless and trembling, I leaned on my elbow in the grass, my eyes wandering aimlessly over the landscape that stretched endlessly before me. I saw the surrounding hills, streaked with golden cornfields, and the winding river snaking far into the distance, weaving between lush green slopes and scattered villages that dotted the horizon like tiny glimmers of light. The forests on the far edge of the scene were faint and dark blue, almost disappearing into the haze, their tops seeming to blend with the shimmering, fiery sky above.

The stillness around me was almost tangible, and the tranquil beauty of the view began to seep into my heart. Slowly, it calmed the storm within me, quieting my racing thoughts. I felt my breathing steady and my chest lighten. Yet, even as I began to feel more at peace, my soul was filled with an unexplainable longing—a sweet, silent yearning that left me both uncertain and strangely fulfilled. It was as though a veil had been lifted from my eyes, allowing me to glimpse something I couldn't yet name. My heart, though still trembling with fear, seemed to reach forward timidly and eagerly toward this unknown feeling, like a child taking its first steps.

Suddenly, a sharp ache welled up in my chest, as though something deep within had been struck. The ache grew and swelled until it overwhelmed me, and I could no longer hold back the flood of tears. But these weren't bitter tears—they were soft, warm, and filled with sweetness. They came from a place I didn't yet understand. Hiding my face in my hands, I surrendered to the feelings coursing through me. My body quivered like a blade of grass swaying in the wind as I gave myself over to this strange, powerful moment.

It was the first time I truly felt my heart awaken, the first time I glimpsed who I was and what I could become. It was as if I had been given a glimpse of the world through new eyes. That moment marked the end of my childhood.

Two hours later, when I returned home, I learned that Madame M. had left. By an unexpected turn of events, she had gone back to Moscow with her husband. I never saw her again.

Thank You for Reading

Dear Reader,

We hope this timeless classic has sparked your imagination and enriched your literary journey. Now that you've turned the final page, we want to share a vision for the future of reading—one where every classic you've ever wanted to explore is at your fingertips, in a format that best suits your life.

We'd like to invite you to gain immediate, unlimited digital & audiobook access to hundreds of the most treasured literary classics ever written—along with the option to secure deluxe paperback, hardcover & box set editions at printing cost. Together, we can spark a new global literary renaissance alongside our small, independent publishing house called "The Library of Alexandria."

Thousands of years ago, the Library of Alexandria stood as a beacon of knowledge—until it was lost to history. We aim to reignite that spirit of preservation and discovery right now, in the modern age—only this time, it's accessible to all, in every language and every format.

Picture a world where every timeless classic, novel, poem, or philosophical treatise is not only available to read but also updated for today's readers—modernized, translated into any language or dialect, and ready to enjoy in any format you choose, whether that is in an eBook, audiobook, paperback, or deluxe hardcover & box set version a printing cost.

By joining our movement to rebuild the modern Library of Alexandria, you become part of an unprecedented mission to offer:

- **Unlimited Audiobook & eBook Access to the Greatest Classics of All Time**

  Instantly explore thousands of legendary works, from Plato and Shakespeare to Jane Austen and Leo Tolstoy. All are instantly ready to read or listen to, giving you a complete literary universe at your fingertips.

- **Paperback & Deluxe Editions at Printing Costs:**

  Purchase any title in a paperback, deluxe hardbound, or deluxe boxset edition at printing costs, shipped right to your doorstep. Curate your personal library of Alexandria with editions worthy of display— crafted to last, designed to captivate, and delivered straight to your door.

- **Modern translations for Contemporary Readers in all languages and dialects**

  Discover a vast selection of classics reimagined in clear, current language—no more struggling with outdated phrases or obscure references. Next to the original versions, we aim to offer translations in as many languages and dialects as possible.

  As we continue our translation efforts and add new languages, readers everywhere can connect with these works as if they were written today. By bridging linguistic divides, you're contributing to ensuring that these timeless stories become more meaningful, accessible, and inspiring for people across the globe.

- **Your Personal Library of Alexandria:**

  Over the months and years, you'll curate a unique physical archive of classics—each volume a testament to your taste, curiosity, and love of knowledge. It's not just about owning books—it's about curating a cultural legacy you'll cherish and pass down for generations to come.

- **Join a Global Literary Renaissance:**

  Your support fuels an ongoing mission: allowing us to reinvest in offering deluxe print editions (including special boxsets) at their true cost, broaden the range of available formats and translations, and extend the reach of these works to new audiences worldwide. By joining today, you're not just preserving a legacy of masterpieces; you set in motion a powerful wave of literary accessibility.

We are more than a publisher—we're a movement, and we can't do it alone. Your support lets us scale our mission, preserving and reimagining history's greatest works for tomorrow's readers.

Become a Torchbearer of knowledge.

Thank you for picking up this book and allowing us into your literary journey. As you turn the pages, know that you're part of something larger: a global effort to keep these stories alive, share their wisdom across borders and generations, and spark a true cultural revival for the modern era.

If this resonates with you—please consider taking the next step by visiting:

www.libraryofalexandria.com

With gratitude and a shared love of knowledge,

The Modern Library of Alexandria Team

Visit:

www.libraryofalexandria.com

Or scan the code below: